MIKAELA
SHIFFRIN

BY JOE TISCHLER

AMICUS LEARNING

Inspire is published by
Amicus Learning, an imprint of Amicus
P.O. Box 227
Mankato, MN 56002
www.amicuspublishing.us

Editor: Aidan Whitcomb and Megan Siewert
Series Designer: Kathleen Petelinsek
Book Designer: Emily Dietz

Library of Congress Cataloging-in-Publication Data
Names: Tischler, Joe, author.
Title: Mikaela Shiffrin / by Joe Tischler.
Description: Mankato, MN : Amicus Learning, an imprint of Amicus, [2025] | Series: Inspire | Includes
   bibliographical references and index. | Audience: Ages 5-9 | Audience: Grades 2-3 | Summary: "Learn
   about Olympics superstar Mikaela Shiffrin and her accomplishments in skiing in this biography packed
   with action photos and fact-filled text suitable for young readers. Includes table of contents, glossary,
   further resources, and index"-- Provided by publisher.
Identifiers: LCCN 2023046024 (print) | LCCN 2023046025 (ebook) | ISBN 9781645499091 (library
   binding) | ISBN 9781645499176 (paperback) | ISBN 9781645499251 (ebook)
Subjects: LCSH: Shiffrin, Mikaela--Juvenile literature. | Skiers--United States--Biography-
   -Juvenile literature. | Women skiers--United States--Biography--Juvenile literature.
Classification: LCC GV854.2.S46 T57 2025 (print) | LCC GV854.2.S46 (ebook)
   | DDC 796.93/5092 [B]--dc23/eng/20231010
LC record available at https://lccn.loc.gov/2023046024
LC ebook record available at https://lccn.loc.gov/2023046025

Photo Credits: Getty/Alain Grosclaude, 4–5, 17, Chet Strange, 18, Doug Pensinger, 9, 12,
13, Ezra Shaw, 14, JURE MAKOVEC, 16, Kevin Mazur, 20, PONTUS LUNDAHL, 6; iStock/
KrizzDaPaul, 1; Shutterstock/chrupka, 7, Fabrizio Malisan, 10–11, JOZEF_KAROLY,
Cover

Printed in China

Table of Contents

Speeding Downhill

Shiffrin dominates the world of alpine skiing.

3, 2, 1...GO! Mikaela Shiffrin bursts out of the gates. She skis fast. She zooms down the mountain. First place!

Shiffrin is one of the best skiers in the world. She has won many Olympic and World Championship medals!

Shiffrin's family continues to support her.

In the Family

Shiffrin comes from a skiing family. Both of her parents raced. Her mother was a great masters racer. She competed in skiing events designed for older adults. Shiffrin's older brother skied on a college team. The whole family skied for fun, too.

GROWING UP WITH SNOW

Mikaela grew up in states known for skiing: Colorado and New Hampshire.

Young Star

Mikaela and her brother went to a ski school. It was in Vermont. It allowed her to race at a young age. By age 14, she was already winning world events.

At just 16 years old, Shiffrin was competing in big ski events like the Aspen Winternational.

Top Racer

Shiffrin races in many **disciplines**. Her best is **slalom**. She has won her most races in that event. She does well in other events, too. These include giant slalom and **downhill**.

Go for Gold

Shiffrin skied in her first Olympics at age 18. It was in 2014. The Winter Games were in Sochi, Russia. She raced in the slalom event. She won the gold medal!

YOUNG CHAMPION
Shiffrin is the youngest slalom winner in Olympic history.

SOCHI 2014

Shiffrin cheers at the end of her giant slalom run at the 2018 Olympics.

More Medals

Shiffrin won another gold medal at the 2018 Pyeongchang Olympics. This was in the giant slalom event. She also won a silver medal. It was in the combined event. The event has downhill and slalom skiing.

Record Holder

Each year in skiing, there is a World Cup, with many races. In March 2023, Shiffrin won her 87th World Cup event. That set a new record for most wins by any alpine skier. By the end of 2023, she had won 91 World Cup events! She has won five World Cup season titles.

WINNING A LOT
By the end of 2023, Shiffrin had won 55 World Cup slalom races. That's the most by a skier in any discipline.

16

KRONPLATZ
Barilla
Audi
ATOMIC
Marlene
PONTE
PLAN DE CORONES

Shiffrin signs autographs for fans after another record-breaking win.

Giving Back

Shiffrin helps a lot of charities. She gave ski goggles to healthcare workers to offer more protection from COVID-19. She also helped create Kindness Wins. This group **advocates** for treating others better. She also speaks to youth about mental health awareness.

ESPY awards are given to pro athletes that have shown excellent performance. The winners are chosen by votes from fans.

THE ESPYS

20

Making Her Mark

Shiffrin is successful in many ways. *Time* magazine named her one of the 100 most influential people of 2023. Also in 2023, she won the ESPY for Best Female Athlete. Shiffrin hopes to keep breaking records in the future.

SUPER STATS

MIKAELA SHIFFRIN

Born: March 13, 1995

Hometown: Edwards, Colorado

Birthplace: Vail, Colorado

AWARDS

Olympic medals: 2 gold, 1 silver

World Championships medals: 14

World Cup event wins: 91, most of all time for alpine skiing

World Cup titles: 2017, 2018, 2019, 2022, 2023

advocate To speak in favor of or recommend publicly.

discipline An event in a sport that focuses on a certain skill or technique.

downhill A skiing event with a small number of turns and extremely fast speeds.

giant slalom A longer, larger, and faster version of a slalom skiing event.

medal An award given to top performers in an athletic competition.

Olympics An international, multi-sport event that takes place every four years.

slalom A skiing event where the skier turns quickly to weave around a course marked by poles.

GLOSSARY

READ MORE

Bolte, Mari. **Mikaela Shiffrin: Olympic Skiing Legend.** North Mankato, Minn.: Capstone Press, 2024.

Gish, Ashley. **Alpine Skiing.** Mankato, Minn.: Creative Education/Creative Paperbacks, 2022.

Hansen, Grace. **Mikaela Shiffrin.** Minneapolis: Abdo Kids Jumbo, 2019.

ON THE WEB

Mikaela Shiffrin Biography, Olympic Medals, and Records
https://olympics.com/en/athletes/mikaela-shiffrin

USA Ski and Snowboard
http://usskiandsnowboard.org/alpine

INDEX

About the Author

Joe Tischler is an editor, sports journalist, and avid sports fan living in Minnesota. He has written about high school, collegiate, and professional games for newspapers. His favorite teams are the Twins, Vikings, Timberwolves, and Golden Gophers.